The Song of My Heartbeat

By Jenn Stoudt

Burton Press International
Attention: Permissions Coordinator
1910 4th Ave E Unit 234
Olympia, WA 98506

ISBN: 978-1-970368-04-8

Cover design by Jennifer Stoudt and Burton Press International

Published by Burton Press International

Dedication

For my mother, who heard this dream before it had a name, and for the daughter I waited decades to hold, whose life made the song complete.

For my husband and our four boys, who have been the rhythm beneath every step. my steady, joyful chorus.

And for the ones who call me “Mom” in their own way, the daughter I didn’t birth but still hold in my heartbeat, and the ones who wandered in and stayed, loved just the same.

Author's Note: A Letter to the Reader

Dear Reader,

This book is a celebration of the sacred bond between a mother and her baby, a connection that begins before the first cry, before the first touch... and doesn't end after the final breath.

From the very beginning, our babies grow within the sound of our hearts. They listen, stretch, and dream inside us, and as they grow, so does our love, expanding in ways we never imagined possible.

Fathers have an irreplaceable position in this journey. Their presence, strength, and steadfast love shape the world our babies are born into and feel safe to explore.

My dad gave me curiosity, humor, and the quiet confidence to keep asking questions, to wonder what I believe and why, to keep searching until I find the answer... and to speak it with confidence.

This story also carries a song of remembrance. My mother gave me my heart, the deep well of love and empathy that flows through every ounce of my being. Before she passed, she heard my vision for this book. She was, as always, my greatest encourager. I still hear her voice and her heartbeat in the quiet moments, just as I hope my children hear mine, guiding them gently as they grow.

A year after my mom's passing, I held the daughter I had prayed for over decades. A little girl who carries a part of her legacy. Her arrival brought unexpected peace and joy into the midst of mourning. She is a quiet echo of all I lost and all I still hold, a living melody of grace and hope.

Congratulations on your new baby. May God bless you and your family as you begin this beautiful new chapter.

Fittingly, the name Carol means joyful song, a reminder that even in sorrow, love still sings.
This story is the song of my heart, and now you can hear it too.

With love,
Jenn Stoudt
(Carol's Daughter)

A Mother's Love Begins

Before you were in my belly,
I loved you more than words could say.
And when I felt you flutter near,
my heart was full of joy and cheer.
A gift, a wish, a tiny spark,
your journey gently found its start.
With every moment spent inside,
you felt my heartbeat as your guide.

BE STILL

Two Hearts Begin to Beat

At just three weeks, your heart began
to flutter soft and strong.
Two little drums, one deep within,
a steady, sacred song
You grew in silence, soft and still,
beneath my skin, unknown.
But every beat you gave to me
was music of my own.

BE STILL

Touch and Movement

You didn't feel the world outside,
but still you felt my care.
I'd press my hand against my skin,
and know that you were there.
Each flutter, stretch, and tiny kick
was like our secret code.
A dance we shared before we met,
on love's invisible road.

BE
STILL

Hearing

By sixteen weeks, you could hear
the life that bloomed around.
My laughter, my voice, my beating heart,
a symphony of sound.
You knew my voice before you saw me,
you moved when I would speak.
The world was soft and far away,
but love was loud and deep.

BE STILL

Sight

Your eyes were closed but full of life,
a world of light and shades of gray.
You blinked and dreamed and sensed the sun,
as colors slipped your way.
Though shadows danced and light drew near,
you couldn't see me clear.
But every beat within my chest
told you, "Have no fear."

Be still

Taste

When I ate something good or strange,
you got to taste it too.
It didn't matter what I chose,
the flavors came to you.
Your tongue began its quiet work,
exploring what I knew.
A tiny taste of life ahead,
was flowing into you.

BE STILL

Sleep

You slept while I would move all day,
with every step you swayed.
But when I finally laid down to rest,
you kicked and softly played.
I sang to you in quiet tones,
before you ever cried.
My body was the song you knew,
that held you safe inside.

Be
Still

Delivery

Then one day, you gave the sign,
your time to come was near.
A signal passed from deep inside,
so gentle, strong, and clear.
We labored close, our strength, our love,
my body knew the way.
You left the world you'd always known,
to see my face that day.

BE
STILL

Into My Arms

You don't hear my heartbeat from inside,
not like you did before.
But now it plays beneath your cheek,
as I hold you close once more.
And when you rest your tiny head
against my skin so near,
you'll find that rhythm once again,
it's still the same, my dear.

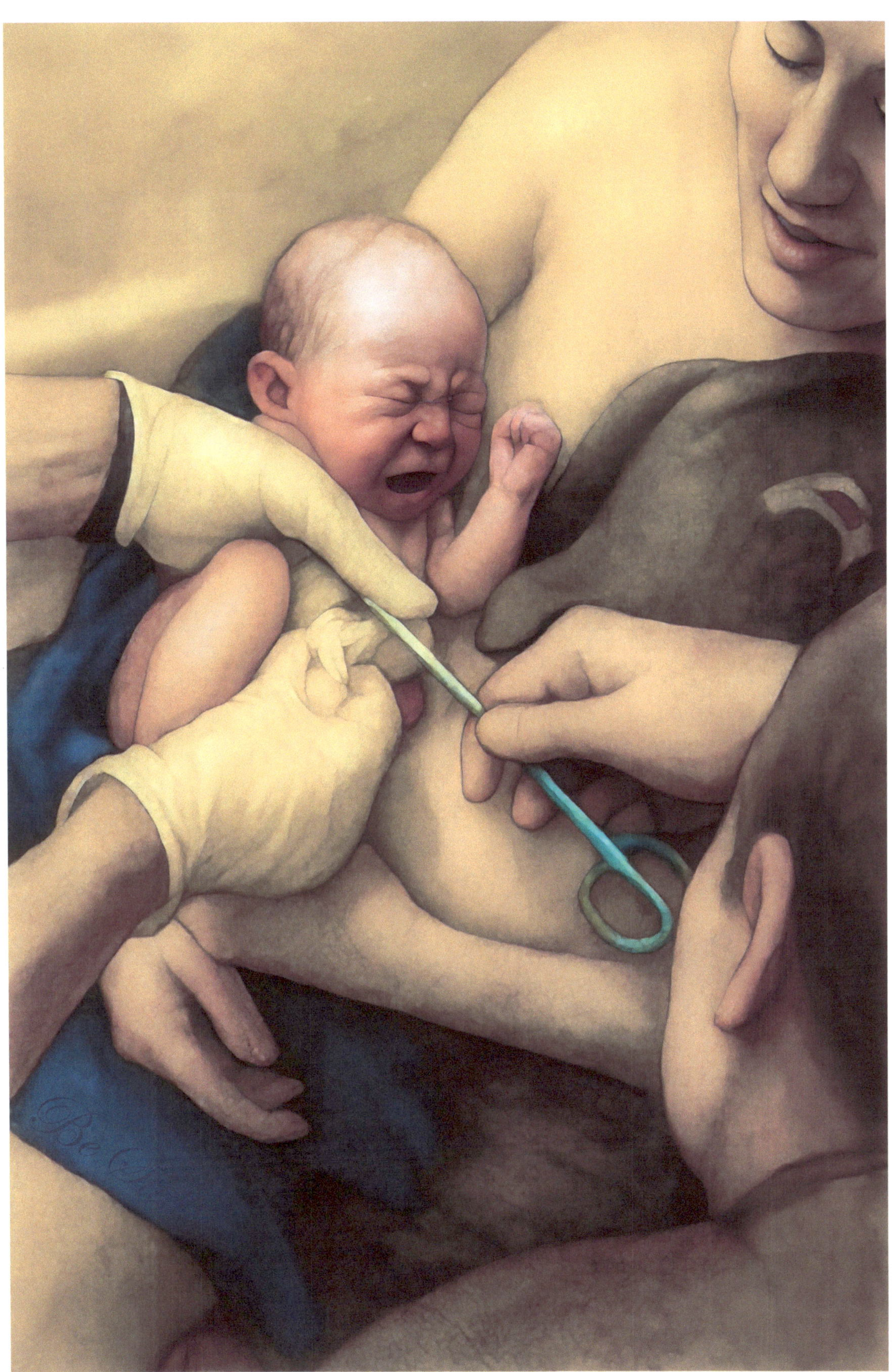

You Are Here

Your daddy holds you close to him,
his voice so soft and low.
You've known us both since long before
we ever said hello.
Now you're here, and in our arms,
we hold you skin to skin.
The love you knew before you came
now lives inside your name.
Your tiny hands curl into ours,
your breath is soft and warm.
The rhythm that you knew so well
still beats to say: you're home.

Be Still

Midnight Nursing

Midnight nursing, oh so sweet,
Won't you, won't you go to sleep?
Your body melts into mine,
Held by love, by God's design.
Off to dreamland, soft and deep,
Nourished well, and held in sleep.
Heavy eyes and fingers still,
Cradled safe within His will.
The world is hushed, the room is small,
But God surrounds and holds us all.
Held together, heart to heart,
Bound in love, we'll never part.
Midnight nursing, hush and glow,
God is in the love we show.
Now rest, my love, the night is clear,
God is with you, always near.

Be Still

Your Baby's Developmental Timeline

Beginning

Beginning → Conceiving Period

Beginning

Dads contribute to the development of the placenta, while moms contribute to a receptive environment where new life can begin. Pre-pregnancy health is important for both men and women.

Implantation

The Egg and Sperm have made a new DNA strand, a whole new person has been created and will begin to implant in the uterus and grow.

First Trimester

1-6 weeks

Heart begins to beat
Brain and nervous system begin forming
Major organ systems start developing.

7-13 weeks

Touch receptors begin forming
Limb development (arms, legs, fingers)
Early movement begins (not yet felt).

Second Trimester

14-20 weeks

Taste buds respond to flavors
Swallowing + sucking begin
Movements become stronger.

21- 27 weeks

Baby can hear:
Mother's voice, Heartbeat, External sounds/music.
"Quickening" - parent begins to feel movement.

Third Trimester

28-35 weeks

Eyes open and respond to light.
Brain development accelerates.
Sleep-wake cycles develop.
REM (dream-like) sleep begins.
Rapid growth and fat storage.

35-41 weeks

Baby moves into birth position (usually head down).
Hormonal signaling between baby & mother.
Baby helps initiate labor.

Fourth Trimester

Hours / Days Old

First breath - lungs expand.
Circulatory shift.
Skin-to-skin regulates:
Temperature, Heart rate, Breathing.
Eyes open briefly. Recognizes mother's scent + voice.

Continued Motherhood

As your baby grows, so do you, learning, stretching, and finding your rhythm together. Lean on your village, and let others hear and support the song of your motherhood.

About the Author

Jennifer Stoudt is a birth doula, childbirth educator, and licensed massage therapist who is passionate about caring for families through every stage and season of life. She believes connection and love begin long before a child is born and continue beyond death. She also believes the body is always communicating, though we are not always taught how to listen.

Through her work, Jennifer creates space for families to slow down, be still, and fully embrace the beauty of this season together.

Inspired by years of supporting parents and witnessing the earliest moments of new life, Jennifer wrote The Heartbeat Song to capture the beauty of a love that begins before the very first heartbeat. It reflects her deep commitment to understanding, supporting, and walking alongside the families she serves.

She lives in Central Texas with her husband and their five children.

The Lord will fight for you; you need only to be still.

—Exodus 14:14

New International Version

www.ingramcontent.com/pod-product-compliance
Lightning Source LLC
LaVergne TN
LVHW070206110826
845147LV00002B/515